Presidents' Day

ALADDIN
An imprint of Simon & Schuster Children's Publishing Division
1230 Avenue of the Americas, New York, NY 10020
First Aladdin paperback edition January 2010
For information about special discounts for bulk purchases, please contact Simon &
Schuster Special Sales at 1-866-506-1949 or business@simonandschuster.com.
The Simon & Schuster Speakers Bureau can bring authors to your live event. For more
information or to book an event contact the Simon & Schuster Speakers Bureau at
1-866-248-3049 or visit our website at www.simonspeakers.com.
Designed by Krista Olsen
The text of this book was set in Century Schoolbook.
Manufactured in the United States of America
1109 LAK
2 4 6 8 10 9 7 5 3 1
Library of Congress Cataloging-in-Publication Data
McNamara, Margaret.
Presidents' Day / by Margaret McNamara ; illustrated by Mike Gordon.
— 1st Aladdin Paperbacks ed.
p. cm. — (Ready-to-read)
Summary: In February, the first-graders in Mrs. Connor's class present
facts about the presidents.
ISBN 978-1-4169-9170-0
[1. Presidents—Fiction. 2. Presidents' Day—Fiction. 3.
Schools—Fiction.] I. Gordon, Mike, 1948 Mar. 16- ill. II. Title.
PZ7.M47879343Pr 2010
[E]—dc22
2009023715

Robin Hill School

Presidents' Day

Written by Margaret McNamara
Illustrated by Mike Gordon

Ready-to-Read
Aladdin Paperbacks
New York   London   Toronto   Sydney

"Who has a birthday soon?"
asked Mrs. Connor.
"I do!" said Ayanna.

"Another famous person
was born on that day,"
said Mrs. Connor.

"You?" asked Michael.

"Abraham Lincoln!"
said Ayanna.

Ayanna knew a lot about
Abraham Lincoln.
"He was a great
president," she said.

"What is a president?"
asked Reza.

All that week the first graders learned about the presidents.

"The president is in charge of America," said Michael.

"Like the principal!" said Reza.

"When we get older,"
said Hannah,
"we will vote to choose
our president."

"*Not* like the principal!"
said Reza.

"The president lives
in the White House,"
said Neil.

"That is a very big house!"
said Jamie.

"The first president was
George Washington,"
said Katie.

"He was good at math,"
said Eigen.

"President Tyler had fifteen children!" said Emma.

"Teddy bears were named
after Teddy Roosevelt,"
said James.

"President Reagan was a movie star before he was a president!" said Becky.

"Our president is
Barack Obama!"
said Nia.

"Abraham Lincoln was tall and a little funny looking," Ayanna said.

"But he was very wise.
He read lots of books."

"He stopped Americans from fighting against one another."

"He thought all people were equal."

"When I grow up,
I want to be a president,
just like Lincoln,"
said Ayanna.

"When you grow up,
I think you will,"
said Mrs. Connor.